TEC

11/06

Y0-BVQ-961

SYMBOLS of AMERICA

The Pledge of Allegiance

Terry Allan Hicks

mc Marshall Cavendish
Benchmark

Marshall Cavendish Benchmark
99 White Plains Road
Tarrytown, New York 10591-9001
www.marshallcavendish.us

Hicks, Terry Allan.
The Pledge of Allegiance / by Terry Allan Hicks.
p. cm. — (Symbols of America)
Summary: "An exploration of the origins and often controversial history of the Pledge of Allegiance"—Provided by publisher.
Includes bibliographical references and index.
ISBN-13: 978-0-7614-2136-8
ISBN-10: 0-7614-2136-X
1. Bellamy, Francis. Pledge of Allegiance to the Flag—History—Juvenile literature.
2. Flags—United States—History—Juvenile literature. I. Title. II. Series.

JC346.I153 2006
323.6'5'0973—dc22
2005020615

Photo research by Anne Burns Images

Front cover photo: Corbis/Steve Chenn
Back cover photo: U.S. Postal Service

The photographs in this book are used by permission and through the courtesy of: *Corbis:* Royalty Free, 1; Bettman, 11; Lindsay Hebbard, 23; Peggy & Ronald Barnett, 27; Chip East/Reuters, 31; Paul A. Souders, 35. *Getty Images:* 4, 20, 32. *Jay Mallin:* 7. *Library of Congress:* 8, 15, 16, 24, 28. *Duke University Special Collections Library:* 12. *National Archives:* 19.

Series design by Adam Mietlowski

Printed in Malaysia

1 3 5 6 4 2

Contents

CHAPTER ONE
Thirty-One Powerful Words   5

CHAPTER TWO
The Story of the Pledge   10

CHAPTER THREE
The Changing Pledge   21

Glossary   36

Find Out More   38

Index   40

Thirty-One Powerful Words

I pledge *allegiance* to the flag of the United States of America and to the *Republic* for which it stands, one Nation under God, *indivisible,* with liberty and justice for all.

These are the words to the Pledge of Allegiance. The pledge is a simple but powerful way for Americans to *express* their *loyalty* to their country. Every morning, about 60 million schoolchildren across the nation *recite* these same thirty-one words.

Students at an elementary school in Texas recite the Pledge of Allegiance.

Many more people, young and old, proudly use the pledge to show their *patriotism* before meetings of the Boy Scouts, the Girl Scouts, the American Legion, and other organizations. Some people—including lawmakers, judges, and religious leaders—have struggled with the question of who should recite the pledge and what, exactly, it should say.

How to Recite the Pledge of Allegiance

The United States Flag Code tells us the proper way to recite the Pledge of Allegiance:

The Pledge of Allegiance . . . should be *rendered* by standing at attention facing the flag with the right hand over the heart. When not in uniform men should remove their head-dress [hats] with their right hand and hold it at the left shoulder, the hand being over the heart. Persons in uniform should remain silent, face the flag, and render the military salute.

The pledge reflects the deep feelings that Americans have for their flag and the country it represents.

The Pledge of Allegiance is very important to Americans, and it has been for many years. This is because the pledge expresses, in a simple but powerful way, the *ideals* on which the United States was founded. And the story of the Pledge of Allegiance—how it came to be such a familiar part of our lives, and how it has changed over the years—is a fascinating one.

◀ *During World War Two, many Japanese Americans—like this young man in Hawaii—took an oath of loyalty to the United States so that they could fight against Japan.*

CHAPTER TWO

The Story of the Pledge

In 1892 the United States was celebrating the four hundredth *anniversary* of Christopher Columbus's first voyage to the Americas. In honor of the event, a special holiday was created. Columbus Day, October 12, was thought to be the date the great explorer landed in the New World.

This illustration shows Christopher Columbus and his crew first coming ashore in the New World. ▶

James Upham was one of the editors of *The Youth's Companion*, a children's magazine published in Boston, Massachusetts. *The Youth's Companion* was a very popular magazine that at one time had more than 500,000 readers. It often worked to encourage patriotism. In 1888 the magazine asked its young readers to send in pennies to buy flags for their schools to display. So many responded that almost 30,000 flags were bought.

Upham decided that the first Columbus Day would be a good time to publish a simple statement of loyalty to be recited by the nation's schoolchildren. The assignment to write this statement was given to another of the magazine's editors, Francis Bellamy.

An advertisement from a 1912 issue of The Youth's Companion.

Francis Bellamy was born in Mount Morris, New York, on May 18, 1855, and raised in Rome, New York. After studying at the University of Rochester and the Rochester Theological Seminary, he became a Baptist minister. He served at churches in Little Falls, New York, and in Boston.

Francis was not the only talented writer in the Bellamy family. One of his cousins, Edward Bellamy, was a famous novelist, best known for *Looking Backward*. It imagined what America would be like in the year 2000—a time that was then far in the future.

Francis Bellamy, author of the Pledge of Allegiance.

▶

PLEDGE TO THE NATION

"I pledge allegiance to the United States of America and to the Flag, Constitution and Democracy for which they uphold; Our Nation, inseparable, with Freedom, Justice and Equality . . . *Forever.*"

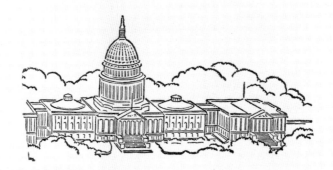

Francis Bellamy responded to James Upham's request by writing the Pledge of Allegiance. But this pledge was different, in small but important ways, from the one Americans recite today. It reads as follows:

I pledge allegiance to my flag and to the Republic for which it stands: one Nation indivisible, with liberty and justice for all.

Did You Know?

When the Pledge of Allegiance was first published, it was unsigned. For many years, James Upham's family claimed he was its true author. In 1939 the United States Flag Association investigated the matter and decided in favor of Francis Bellamy. In 1957 the Library of Congress came to the same conclusion. Although the pledge was Upham's idea, it is now widely accepted that it was Bellamy who actually wrote it.

◀ *A different pledge of loyalty to America, printed in 1941.*

The Pledge of Allegiance was published in the September 8, 1892, issue of *The Youth's Companion.* It quickly caught the nation's attention. President Benjamin Harrison issued a *proclamation* calling for a special ceremony for saluting the flag to be added to the Columbus Day celebrations. An important part of this ceremony was the new Pledge of Allegiance. *The Youth's Companion* sent *leaflets* including the pledge to schools across the country. On October 12, 1892, more than 12 million children recited it nationwide.

The Pledge of Allegiance was on its way to becoming a key part of Americans' everyday lives. Before long, most people could recite the words by heart. But there were still important changes ahead.

Benjamin Harrison, president of the United States from 1889 to 1893. ▶

CHAPTER THREE
The Changing Pledge

The changes that have been made to the Pledge of Allegiance over the past century show how important the pledge is to the American people.

The first change came on June 14, 1923, at the National Flag Conference in Washington, D.C. The words "my Flag" were changed to "the Flag of the United States." The reason: America was then, as it is now, a land of *immigrants*. Some people were concerned that immigrants might think the pledge was talking about the flags of the countries they had left when they came to America. The following year, the wording was changed again, to read "the flag of the United States of America."

◀ *Some members of a soccer team pledge allegiance before a game. Others—those who are not American citizens—do not.*

Francis Bellamy was not asked about these changes. Some people say he was unhappy about them. But they became an accepted part of the pledge.

Over the first half of the 1900s, the Pledge of Allegiance grew in popularity. But despite the fact that millions of people were reciting the pledge, it was not officially recognized by the United States government until June 22, 1942. That was when the pledge was added to the United States Flag Code. It is a set of rules that state how the country's official symbols, such as the American flag and the Great Seal of the United States, should be treated and honored.

Two Native American men—Kiowa veterans—show the proper way to fold the American flag.

By that time, many state and local governments had passed laws that required all schoolchildren to recite the Pledge of Allegiance. Many people believed that this was wrong. They included the Jehovah's Witnesses, a religious group whose members believe they should swear allegiance only to God. They challenged a West Virginia law that forced students to recite the pledge.

Schoolchildren in Connecticut give the original "Bellamy salute" in 1942.

Did You Know?

At first, people often recited the pledge while giving the "Bellamy salute," with the right arm raised stiffly. Later, many people were troubled by its similarity to the fascist salute used in Germany and Italy—countries the United States fought in World War Two. So the salute was replaced by the now-familiar right hand held over the heart.

25

On June 14, 1943, the United States Supreme Court ruled that requiring anyone to recite the pledge was a *violation* of the United States Constitution.

The Constitution, created at the Constitutional Convention in Philadelphia in 1787, outlines the basic *principles* on which the United States government is based. The First Amendment to the Constitution *guarantees* that all Americans have certain rights—including the right to speak freely and the right to practice their religion. The Supreme Court decided if people were forced to recite the Pledge of Allegiance, they would lose their rights under the First Amendment. The court's ruling stands to this day.

The Constitution of the United States, another important symbol of America. ▶

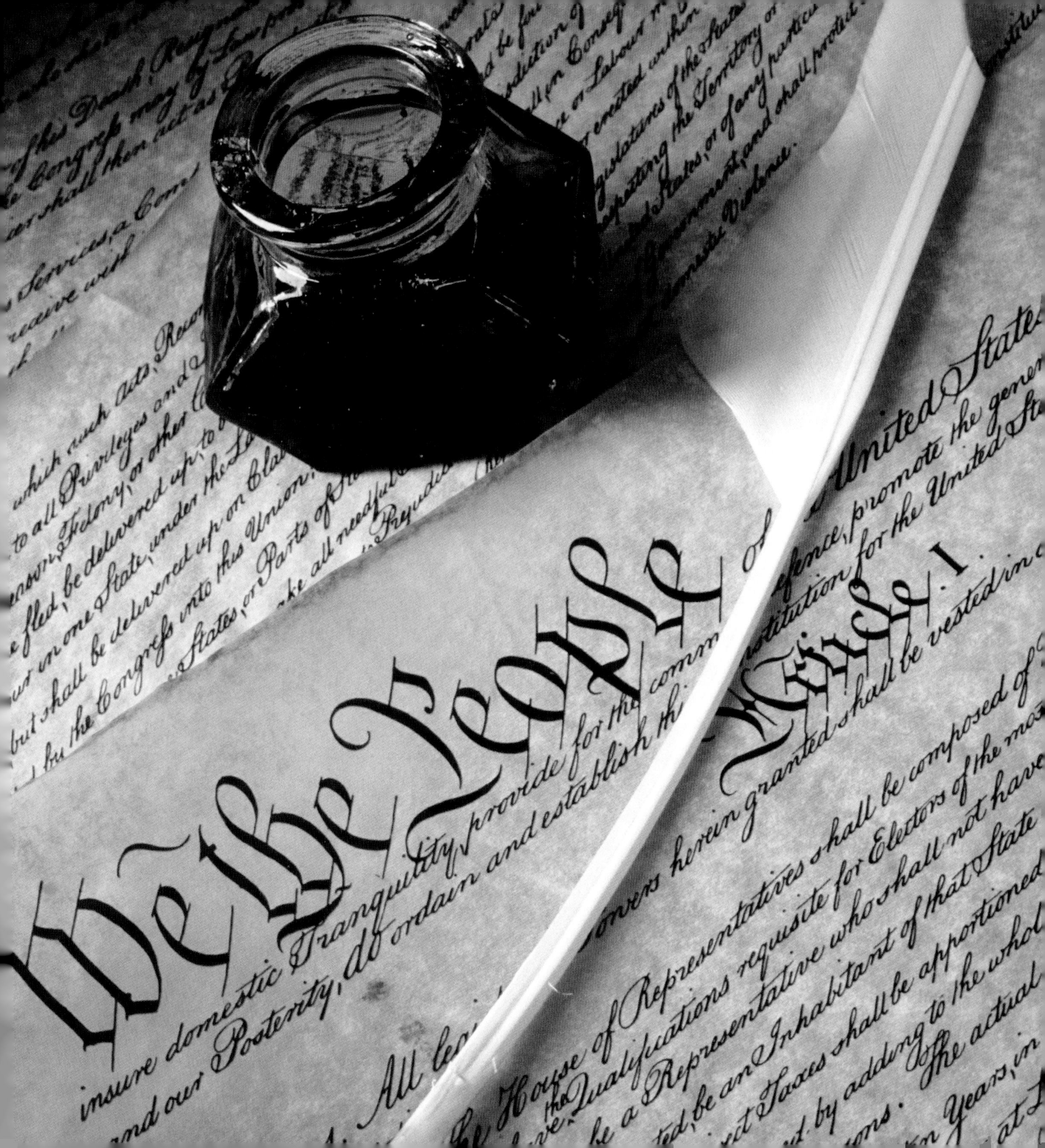
We the People

The latest change to the Pledge of Allegiance was the one that has been most seriously debated. It came in the mid–1950s. This was a time when many Americans were worried about what they saw as the threat of *communism*. Some people believed that, to answer that threat, the Pledge of Allegiance should express a belief in religion. In many Communist countries, such as the Soviet Union, people were not allowed to practice their religions freely.

Children pledge allegiance to the flag as part of a program presented during World War Two.

To show that America did not support communism, some people asked that the wording of the Pledge of Allegiance be changed to "one nation, under God, indivisible." Others *objected*, but President Dwight D. Eisenhower made this change official on June 14, 1954.

Since then, some Americans have continued to oppose the change. They believe the mention of God goes against the idea that government and religion should be separated and should not mix. Still others argue that this phrase simply expresses America's religious *traditions*.

A new American citizen—an immigrant from the North African nation of Morocco—recites the Pledge of Allegiance for the first time.

On June 26, 2002, a *federal* court in California made an important decision about this phrase. The court said that reciting the Pledge of Allegiance with the words "under God" in schools violated the Constitution. Some Americans were pleased with the ruling, but many others were not. More than a hundred members of Congress gathered on the steps of the Capitol, in Washington, D.C., to recite the pledge—including the words "under God"—to protest the court's decision.

◀ *A man protests a court ruling in a case about the Pledge of Allegiance.*

These disagreements show that, even after more than a century, the Pledge of Allegiance still stirs deep, heartfelt feelings. As America has changed, so has the pledge. It is still a great symbol of a nation where people are free to express their opinions, and to discuss issues they disagree about. Francis Bellamy would surely be proud of the important place his simple but powerful words have taken in the lives of Americans today.

"I pledge allegiance to the flag of the United States of America . . ." Can you recite the rest?

Glossary

allegiance—Loyalty; for example, to one's country.

anniversary—The annual return of an important date such as a birthday.

communism—A political and social system in which goods are shared or owned in common by a group.

express—To say what you think or feel.

federal—The government of the entire United States.

guarantee—To make sure, to promise.

ideal—An important belief or guiding principle.

immigrant—Someone who moves permanently to a different country.

indivisible—Impossible to tear apart.

leaflet—A printed paper with information, usually handed out for free.

loyalty—Remaining true to a person, a country, or a belief.

object—To disagree with something; a verb.

patriotism—The love of one's country.

principle—A basic idea or rule of conduct.

proclamation—An official announcement.

recite—To repeat from memory or to say out loud.

render—To make, create, or do.

republic—A government of elected leaders chosen by the people.

tradition—A belief or a custom that has existed for a long time.

violation—The breaking of a law or rule.

Find Out More

Books

Fata, Heather. *The Pledge of Allegiance.* New York: Rosen, 2003.

Kallen, Stuart A. *The Pledge of Allegiance.* Chanhassan, MN: Abdo, 1994.

Kozleski, Lisa. *The Pledge of Allegiance.* Broomall, PA: Mason Crest Publishers, 2003.

Swanson, June. *I Pledge Allegiance.* Minneapolis: Lerner, 2002.

Webster, Christine. *The Pledge of Allegiance.* Danbury, CT: Children's Press, 2003.

West, Delno C., and Jean M. West. *Uncle Sam and Old Glory: Symbols of America.* New York: Atheneum Books for Young Readers, 2000.

Web Sites

A Matter of Conscience
http://www.loc.gov/exhibits/treasures/trr006.html

National Flag Day Foundation—The Story of the Pledge of Allegiance
http://www.flagday.org/Pages/StoryofPledge.html

The Original Pledge of Allegiance
http://www.usflag.org/history/pledgeofallegiance.html

The Pledge of Allegiance—A Short History
http://history.vineyard.net/pledge.htm

Time magazine for Kids—Pledge of Allegiance under Fire
http://www.timeforkids.com/TFK/news/story/0,6260,266506,00.html

Index

Page numbers in **boldface** are illustrations.

American Legion, 6

Bellamy, Edward, 14
Bellamy, Francis, 13, 14, **15**, 17, 22, 34
Bellamy salute, **24**, 25
Boston, 13, 14
Boy Scouts, 6

Capitol, U.S., 33
Columbus, Christopher, 10, **11**
Columbus Day, 10, 13, 18
communism, 29, 30
Congress, 33
Constitution, U.S., 26, **27**, 30
Constitutional Convention, 26
court, federal, 33

Eisenhower, Dwight D., 30

First Amendment, 26
flags, 13, 17, 21, 22
freedom of religion, 26, 29
freedom of speech, 26, 34

Germany, 25
Girl Scouts, 6, **7**
governments, 18, 22, 25, 26, 30
Great Seal, the, 22

Harrison, Benjamin, 18, **19**

immigrants, 21, 30, **31**
Italy, 25

Jehovah's Witnesses, 25

laws and lawmakers, 6, 25
Library of Congress, 17
Looking Backward, 14
loyalty oath, **8**, 9, 13

National Flag Conference, 21
Native Americans, 22, **23**
New World, 10

patriotism, 6, 13
Philadelphia, 26
Pledge of Allegiance
    changes to, 21, 22, 29, 30
    court rulings on, 26, 33

Pledge of Allegiance
    history of, 13, 17, 18, 22, 26
    how to recite, 6, 25
    versions of, **16**, 17
    words to, 5, 17, 21

religion, 6, 25, 26, 29, 30
Rochester
    Theological Seminary, 14
    University of, 14

schoolchildren, **4**, 5, 13, 18, **24**, 25, **28**
Soviet Union, 29
Supreme Court, U.S., 26

United States Flag
    Association, 17
United States Flag Code, 6, 22
Upham, James, 13, 17

Washington, D.C., 21, 33
World War Two, 9, 25, 29

Youth's Companion, The, **12**, 13, 18